4. A cygnet is a baby . . ?
A - seal B - swan C - otter

5. Do you know the name of this large bird?
A — stork B — ostrich C — turkey

6. One of these migrates every year to spend the winter in Africa. Is it . . ?
A - panda B - hedgehog C - swallow

7. This animal is an . . ?
A - antelope B - armadillo C - anteater

Now turn to the back of the book.

Printed and Published by D. C. Thomson & Co., Ltd., Dundee and London.

Toys

Girls and Boys,

There are lots of lovely stories and exciting things to do in Little Star Book. I know you'll enjoy reading about Mrs Hedgehog's Bonnet, Mervyn's magic muddle, Kandy Kangaroo and Ring-a-ling Rosie.

You will also find **Puzzles** and an exciting **Game** to play.

Happy reading!

Jenny learns to skate

JENNY DUCKLING popped her head up out of her warm nest. It had been a cold night and she was feeling hungry. "I'll swim across the pond and look for breakfast," she thought.

2 — But, when Jenny put her foot into the water, she gasped. "What's happened?" she cried in amazement. "The water's all cold and hard!"

"Oh, dear!" said Jenny's brother, Jeremy. "It's ice! The water has frozen. When the children come into the park to feed us, we'll be stuck on this island. We won't be able to swim across for bread."

The other ducklings gathered around, shaking their heads, and quacking sadly.

"Perhaps, if we call out, someone will bring us some food," suggested Jenny.

So all the ducklings began to jump around, flapping their wings and quacking loudly.

But the children thought they were playing and just waved back to them.

3 — As the morning wore on, the birds began to feel hungrier and hungrier. "We'll have to think of something," Jeremy said. "I'm starving."

"Please, Jenny," the other ducklings quacked. "Please think of something."

"I've a splendid idea!" Jenny cried at last. She leaned over and pecked at the ice with her strong beak. But the ice refused to break.

As Jenny slipped and slithered around, however, she spotted some children on the far side of the lake. They were acting very strangely.

4 — "The children aren't on the paths today," she quacked. "Look — they're walking on the water, with funny, long slidey steps!"

Jenny sat down and watched how the children moved. "If I could take slidey steps like that, I could glide across the water, too," Jenny thought. She struggled to her feet again and tried to skate on the ice, like the children were doing.

5 — When Milly Moorhen saw what Jenny was trying to do, she thought it looked easy. But, when she came running down the bank, her little feet slipped from underneath her and she landed on her tail with a bump!

"Let me show you!" Jenny called.

For, by now, Jenny was beginning to take long, gliding steps.

"I can do it — I can do it!" she quacked happily.

"It's easy for you because of your wide, webbed feet," Milly croaked, wishing her feet were as big as Jenny's.

6 — One by one, the other ducklings waddled on to the ice and Jenny taught them how to slide along so they wouldn't fall.

"I'm sure if we all stayed together we could get across to the children," she said. "Come along, Jeremy. You hold on to me. You others hold on to Jeremy."

Very slowly, the little line of skating ducklings began to move across the ice.

7 — "Patty, come and look at the ducks!" one of the children called suddenly to her friend. "They're *skating* across the lake towards us!"

"I've brought some bread," said Patty and pulled out a large paper bag.

As the ducklings reached them, the children broke up the bread and laid it on the ice. Hungrily the ducks began to eat.

All except Jenny, that is.

"Jenny's forgotten about being so hungry, now that she's learned how to skate on ice," laughed Milly. "Just look at her!"

"We'll keep some crumbs for her," grinned Jeremy. "If she hadn't learned to skate *none* of us would have had any breakfast this morning."

Peter Puppy's new home

IN the window of the pet shop
  Sat a puppy, Pete,
Watching all the laughing children
  Walking in the street.

2 — Every day, wee Sue and Jamie
  Made a special stop—
Pressed their noses to the window
  Of their favourite shop.

3 — One day, Mummy came there with them
  And they walked inside.
"We have saved a lot of money,"
  Jamie said with pride.

4 — "May we see the puppy, Peter?"
  Sue said, with a smile.
From the window, lady took him,
  For a little while.

5 — They had not enough to buy him,
    So they went away.
Cleaned Dad's car and dug the garden,
    Shopped for Mum each day.

6 — Soon they'd earned a lot more money.
    Put it in a jar.
In the pet shop, asked the lady,
    "Count what coins there are."

7 — "Now you have enough," she told them,
    So they bought young Pete.
Put a lead and collar on him.
    Looked so smart and neat.

8 — Mummy bought a bowl and basket,
    Then they took him home.
Loved and fed and warm and happy,
    Pete will never roam!

The lost letter

TOMMY was one of Santa's little helpers. He had spent lots of time helping Santa to make toys for Christmas, in the hope of being allowed to deliver them on Christmas Eve.

However, poor Tommy had caught a bad cold and was being left behind to tidy the workshop.

He felt very sad as he watched Santa and his happy friends setting off into the night in the big sleigh.

Tommy was very friendly though, and he decided not to sulk. Instead, he began to tidy the workshop.

When Tommy lifted the piles of tinsel off the floor, he came across an envelope. Tommy couldn't help noticing the envelope, because it was bright orange. It was addressed to Santa Claus.

Dear Santa, orange
is my favourite
colour. Please may
I have an orange
pedal car for
christmas?
Thank you,
from Billy Banks xx
for my mummy
olates y mummy
ddy?

Tommy quickly opened the letter. It was from a little boy, named Billy, whose favourite colour was orange. Billy was hoping to receive an orange pedal car from Santa.

"Oh, dear!" gasped Tommy. "This letter must have been lost."

Tommy decided to find an orange pedal car for Billy in the workshop.

He ran to the pedal car cupboard. But there were no *orange* pedal cars to be seen.

"I know!" exclaimed Tommy. "I'll *paint* one of these cars orange."

Tommy marched to the paint cupboard to fetch a tin of orange paint. There were lots of cans of every colour, but, sadly, there were no tins of orange paint left.

"What will I do?" Tommy sighed, desperately. "Billy will be so disappointed if he doesn't get an orange pedal car." Then Tommy remembered something which he had learned in his art lessons.

You see, red paint mixed with yellow becomes *orange* paint. Tommy quickly mixed the red and yellow paint together, until he ended up with a can of bright orange paint.

He chose a yellow pedal car and started painting. Soon, Tommy had turned the yellow pedal car into a beautiful, bright orange car.

Tommy stood back to admire his work.
Just then, Santa and the helpers returned home. Tommy told Santa about Billy's letter being lost. Santa *was* pleased with Tommy's thoughtfulness for Billy.

Billy's present was wrapped in bright orange paper and put in the sleigh.
"It's very lucky that you found Billy's letter," Santa grinned at Tommy. "Now, how can I reward you for all your hard work?"

Santa immediately thought of a good way to reward the kind helper. He let Tommy come with him to deliver Billy's present. Tommy was even allowed to steer the sleigh.
"This is the best Christmas present *I* could ever wish for!" Tommy called, proudly.

Penguin puzzle-time

Colour this picture, using your paints or crayons.

There are six differences between these penguin pictures. Can you find them?

Help this penguin through the maze to find the hole in the ice.

Can you tell which two penguins are exactly alike?

Then try to find six snowflakes hidden on this page.

The little tree goblin

LUCY had a special tree in her garden. It had a smooth patch on the bark which Lucy thought looked just like a door.

One day, Lucy bounced her ball against the tree.

"Who did that?" asked a grumpy voice.

Lucy was amazed to see a little man pushing open the smooth bark!

"Are you an elf?" asked Lucy.

"Certainly not!" exclaimed the little man.. "I am a tree goblin and my name is Greencap. I have to tell the tree what season it is."

"You *do* have an important job," said Lucy.

Greencap was pleased to hear that and let Lucy peep inside his house. It looked very cosy.

"Don't you get lonely by yourself?" asked Lucy.

"Oh, no!" laughed Greencap. "I can visit the other tree goblins. Come on! I'll show you where they live."

So Lucy carried Greencap round the garden and the little goblin showed her where his chums lived.

"They won't come out," he said. "They're very shy."

Then Greencap looked at his watch.

"Goodness!" he cried. "I must be going!"

As Greencap dashed away, he dropped his hat. Lucy hung it on a branch and, next morning, it was gone.

Lucy never saw Greencap again, but, every time she passed the tree, she knocked, just in case he was in!

Ellie helps out

1 — Ellie, the elephant, lived in a zoo. Usually, she liked the zoo, but today she was feeling bored. "I wish I had someone to play with," she sighed.

2 — "It's all right for the monkeys," she continued. "There are lots of them. There's only *one* of me!" Just then, Ellie's keeper came into her enclosure.

3 — "I'll have fun with my keeper," thought Ellie. She grabbed his broom and started to play tug-o'-war. The keeper, however, wasn't in a very good mood.

4 — "Let go!" the keeper shouted. "All right!" giggled Ellie. She let go of the brush suddenly and the keeper fell backwards. The monkeys screamed with laughter.

5 — The keeper didn't think it was funny and stormed out of Ellie's enclosure. Then Ellie noticed he hadn't locked the gate. "I'm going for a walk," she decided.

6 — Ellie wandered over to the monkeys' cage for a chat. "Why don't you turn on that hose?" chattered the monkeys. "That will be fun."

7 — "Ooh, yes!" laughed Ellie and hurried over to the hose. She curled her trunk round the tap and turned it. The water squirted all over the place as the hose twisted and jerked about.

8 — Two keepers dashed up to turn off the hose. They were very angry. Ellie realised she was in trouble. "I'm off!" she thought.

9 — Ellie dashed out of the zoo. She hadn't gone very far along the road, when she saw the zoo van stuck in the soft grass verge.

10 — Ellie didn't wait to think. She climbed into the ditch beside the grass verge and pushed the van with all her might. It slowly moved back on to the road.

11 — The zoo keepers were very pleased with Ellie and forgave her for her naughty pranks. "I must find you something interesting to do," said her keeper.

12 — So the keeper strapped a special seat to Ellie's back. Now Ellie could give rides to the children who came to the zoo. "I won't get bored again," Ellie smiled.

Mrs Hedgehog's Bonnet

MRS HEDGEHOG was really excited. It was the day of the Easter bonnet parade and Mrs Hedgehog had just finished decorating her bonnet. She covered it with daffodils and green leaves.

Then Mrs Hedgehog left the bonnet on the kitchen table, while she hurried upstairs to tidy her twins' bedrooms.

At that moment, the twins, who were called Harry and Hannah, came in with their friend, Gary Goat.

"I'm hungry," said Hannah. So she fetched some biscuits.

"I don't like biscuits!" cried Gary, as he caught sight of Mrs Hedgehog's bonnet. "But I just love green leaves." And he began to eat the Easter bonnet decorations!

Just then, Mrs Hedgehog came in.

"Stop!" she wailed. "You're eating my bonnet!"

Well, Gary *did* feel sorry about ruining the bonnet. He and the twins went out into the garden.

"Poor Mummy," sighed Hannah. "She was so looking forward to taking part in the Easter bonnet parade."

"Couldn't we decorate the bonnet with something else?" suggested Gary. "After all, I only ruined the leaves and flowers." But no one could think of anything else to use.

Just then, Mrs Sparrow flew past.

"Hello, twins!" she called. "Is your mother in?" The twins nodded.

"Good," Mrs Sparrow went on. "I wonder if she will look after my nest and eggs while I do some shopping?"

Kind Mrs Hedgehog agreed to look after the nest.

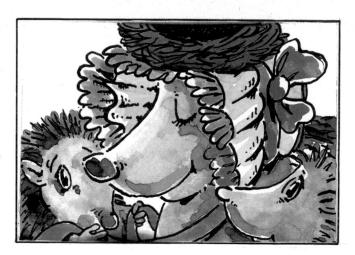

"That's it!" cried Harry, when Mrs Sparrow had gone. "We could borrow the nest for a little while and use it to decorate Mummy's Easter bonnet." So that's just what they did.

"Try it on, Mummy," urged Hannah excitedly. Mrs Hedgegog put the bonnet on her head. It looked awful!

"Oh, dear!" she thought to herself. "That nest makes my bonnet look so untidy. But I don't want to disappoint the twins. I'll pretend I think my bonnet is very smart now." So that's what she told Harry and Hannah.

"Good," smiled the twins. "Now we can all go to the Easter parade."

At the parade, there were lots of lovely decorated bonnets.

At last, the judge was ready to announce the winner for the best Easter bonnet.

"The runner-up is Mrs Hen," called out Mrs Owl. Everyone clapped and cheered. Mrs Hedgehog hoped no one had noticed her terrible bonnet!

"Now for the winner," went on Mrs Owl. "This year, the first prize goes to Mrs Hedgehog for her unusual bonnet with nest and baby chicks."

"What baby chicks?" gasped the twins.

Sure enough, peering over the side of the nest were four baby chicks, newly hatched from their eggs! "What a super bonnet!" everyone cried. Mrs Hedgehog *was* pleased — and so were the twins. Especially when they saw Mummy had won a huge box of chocolates and a bunch of daffodils!

"Let's go home now," smiled Mrs Hedgehog.

"It *was* a super Easter bonnet, wasn't it, Mummy?" smiled Harry and Hannah.

"Yes, dears," agreed Mrs Hedgehog. "In fact, it was the best Easter bonnet I've ever seen!"

Jack and the broomstick

JACK, the pixie, *was* cross.

"Work, work, work!" he moaned. "There's so much to do in this garden, I never have any time to play."

Suddenly, an old woman appeared in front of Jack. She wore a cloak, a green, pointed hat and red, sparkly shoes.

"What do you want?" Jack snapped.

"I've come to help you," said the old woman. "Even the Fairy Queen has heard how bad-tempered you've become."

Jack told the old woman how tired he was, looking after the queen's garden.

"What you need is some transport," said the old woman. "I'll lend you my broomstick."

Then, without another word, the old woman vanished, and only her broomstick remained!

"How can a broomstick help?" complained Jack.

"Come here!" he cried. "I need your help." But the broomstick took no notice.

Jack began to feel even more bad-tempered. He tried to grab hold of the broom. But it hopped away!

Jack ran after the broom and tried to sit on it. However, the broom flew up into the air whenever Jack went near it.

"I give up!" shouted Jack. "I thought that old woman wanted to help me."

Then Jack began to smile, when he remembered how funny the old woman had looked.

Suddenly, the broomstick hopped a little nearer to Jack.

Now Jack knew how to make the broomstick obey him.

"I have to be nice and *smile!*" he said.

So, Jack gave a huge smile and said politely, "Please come here, Broomstick."

At once, the broomstick marched over to Jack.

"Right," Jack grinned, "*please* fly me over the garden." The broom did as the pixie asked.

Jack had great fun, sailing over the Fairy Queen's garden. But, when he wanted to stop the broom, he forgot to be polite.

"Put me down!" he snapped. Instead of obeying Jack, the broomstick zoomed higher into the air!

"I'm sorry!" gasped Jack.

With that, the broom slowed down.

"Well done, Jack!" called a voice. It was the Fairy Queen!

Suddenly, Jack saw the queen was wearing a pair of sparkly shoes — the old woman had been the queen in magic disguise!

When he looked up, the Fairy Queen had vanished.

Well, after that, Jack learned his lesson. He even began to enjoy his work in the garden — especially since he had a flying broomstick to help him!

The wild west wind

1 — Mrs Mouse and Mr Squirrel lived on the edge of Fernhill Forest. One day, they were both doing their chores. Mrs Mouse's children, Kim and Tim, played nearby.

2 — Mrs Mouse was hanging up her clean sheets and Mr Squirrel was busily sweeping up the fallen leaves. "I'm going to burn these leaves later!" he called.

3 — Mrs Mouse took her children indoors for a snack. But she hadn't noticed how the west wind had risen, until Kim pointed at the swirling leaves outside.

4 — Mrs Mouse hurried to her door. "My washing will blow away!" she cried. Mr Squirrel was also upset, because his neat pile of leaves was now being blown all around.

5 — Oliver Owl, the wizard, had been watching. "Why don't you *catch* the wind?" he said. "But how?" gasped Mrs Mouse. "I'll give you a magic sack," grinned the wizard.

6 — So that's exactly what Mrs Mouse and Mr Squirrel did. They took the wizard's sack and ran round and round, catching the wild west wind inside it.

7 — The bag filled up like a balloon. "Hooray!" called Mrs Mouse. "We've caught the wind!" She tied up the sack, before the wind could escape.

8 — "Now that the wind has been captured, I can sweep up my leaves again," chuckled Mr Squirrel. But Kim and Tim weren't so happy. Without the breeze, they couldn't fly their kites.

9 — Mrs Mouse and Mr Squirrel soon found that they needed the wind, too. Her sheets wouldn't dry and his bonfire smoke wouldn't blow away.

10 — Mrs Mouse and Mr Squirrel began to argue. Neither of them noticed Oliver Owl magically opening the sack and letting the wind escape. At once, it started to blow again.

11 — This time, Mrs Mouse and Mr Squirrel were delighted to see the wind. It carried Mr Squirrel's bonfire smoke high into the sky, and it quickly dried Mrs Mouse's washing!

12 — "We can play with our kites," grinned Kim. "Thanks, Oliver Owl," giggled Mrs Mouse. "We won't try to catch the wind again, now we know how helpful it can be."

King Reggie's royal band

KING REGGIE and his good queen, Nell,
Are having quite a ball.
They're entertaining everyone
Inside the palace hall.

"Let dancing start!" King Reggie calls.
But then, a little page,
Bows low and says, "The band's not here."
The king's in quite a rage!

"Now, now, dear husband," says Queen Nell.
"You know how well we play,
With saucepan, board and scrubbing brush,
So let us save the day."

The king strips off his royal coat.
They bring the saucepans in.
Then he, the queen and "palace band"
Make such a lovely din!

The dancing dolls

"CUCKOO!" cried the little bird, five times, as it popped out of the clock.

Mr Trim, the toy maker, looked at the time.

"Five o'clock," he sighed. "Time to go home." The old man reached for his coat and hat and put them on.

He had no sooner left the shop, when the toys came to life!

"Mr Trim has gone!" they said to each other. "What games will we play tonight?"

The toys climbed off the shelves and looked at each other.

"I know!" cried Candy, the disco dancing doll. "Let's do some disco dancing."

The other toys didn't want to do that, but they knew Candy could be nasty if she didn't get her own way.

The disco doll looked at Victor, the musical doll.

"You can play for me!" she snapped.

Just then, another doll climbed down from the shelf. She was called Drina, and she was a ballerina doll.

Mr Trim had made Drina a long time ago and now her dress was very tatty.

"I'd love to do some dancing," she told Victor. "Would you play for me, too?"

Well, when Candy heard that, she began to laugh unkindly.

"Who wants to watch a grubby looking doll like you!" she cried. "I'm the only dancing doll around here."

Victor felt sorry for Drina. She was a very kind doll and she never said anything to hurt the other toys.

"I'll play for you, Drina," promised Victor.

Meanwhile, the other toys were beginning to play their own games.

Co-co, the juggling clown, was showing the others how to juggle.

"They're so busy watching that silly Co-co, they won't watch me," thought Candy.

The naughty doll tip-toed over to Co-co and stuck out her foot!

Poor Co-co didn't see Candy's foot and he tripped over it.

"You're not very good," giggled Candy. "But watch me, everyone."

Candy began to do some disco steps.

"She *is* good," agreed the toys.

Then it was Drina's turn to dance.

Well, the toys had never seen anyone dance so beautifully as Drina.

"She's wonderful!" cheered the toys.

Just then, Teddy caught sight of Mr Trim passing the shop window.

"Quick, everyone!" he cried. "Mr Trim is coming!"

The toys dashed back to the shelves. In the rush, poor Drina was knocked over. Victor stayed behind to help Drina up from the floor.

However, by now, Mr Trim had come into the shop. He'd forgotten something.

The old man caught sight of Victor and Drina sitting on the floor.

Mr Trim picked up the two dolls and took them home.

Next morning, Mr Trim arrived at the shop with Victor and Drina.

Drina was wearing a beautiful, long, white dress and Victor looked smart in a new suit.

Mr Trim put the dolls on top of a cardboard wedding cake.

"There!" he said. "These dolls are just right for the wedding display in my window."

The other toys thought so, too.

Even Candy had to agree that Drina and Victor *did* look very smart.

Take your place, for the... Monkey

9
8
7
6
5
4
3
2
1
start

9
8
7
6
5
4
3
2
1
start

Trace this monkey pointer on to card. You will need four of them for each player.

Cut along the dotted lines on the leaves to make a "home" for each monkey.

race

To play this exciting game, you will need two to four players, a dice and four "monkeys" for each player. Each player chooses a tree.

Throw the dice to decide who goes first. Then, next throw, start to race! Move your monkey pointers, one at a time, up the tree. The first person with all four monkeys in the slots at the top of their tree, is the winner.

9
8
7
6
5
4
3
2
1
start

9
8
7
6
5
4
3
2
1
start

Mervyn's magic muddle

MERVYN was a very kind-hearted wizard who liked to use his magic powers to help people. One day, when Mervyn was out for a walk, Granny Goldie came running towards him.

"Can you help me, Mervyn?" she asked. "You see, my chimney needs cleaned."

"Of course I'll help," said Mervyn.

The only trouble was, Mervyn had lost his spell book! Mervyn racked his brains for a chimney sweeping spell.

"I remember it!" he cried, at last. "Or, at least, I *think* I can remember it! Anyway, here goes."

Mervyn cast his spell and, at once, there was a loud shriek from the cottage. The next minute, Granny Goldie came rushing out, chased by an angry-looking chimney brush!

"Oh, dear!" wailed Mervyn. "Perhaps that wasn't the right spell after all. Sorry, Granny — and, er, ta-ta!"

"Now where can my spell book have got to?" puzzled Mervyn, as he walked on home through the forest. Mervyn was so busy thinking, that he nearly fell over his cat, Slinky Joe.

"Why don't you look where you're going?" Mervyn cried crossly.

"What a cheek!" grumbled Slinky Joe and started walking away in a huff.

"Oh, I'm sorry," said Mervyn. "It's just that I've lost my spell book and I can't get my spells right without it."

"Well, *I* haven't got it," sniffed Slinky Joe. "So there's no need to snap at me!"

Mervyn and Slinky Joe walked on towards home. Suddenly, Mervyn gasped in horror.

"Look!" he cried. "The moon has turned blue!"

Then the moon spotted Mervyn.

"Ah!" he thundered. "I've been looking for you, Mervyn. You're the only wizard around here, so *you* must have turned me blue. Well I don't think it's very funny, so please *turn me yellow again*!"

"But I didn't do anything!" spluttered Mervyn. He was very worried now. Somebody must have been using his book to play tricks.

Just then, Slinky Joe caught sight of two small figures running towards them.

The figures turned out to be two little girls. One of them was carrying a large book. Mervyn recognised it immediately.

"My spell book!" he cried.
"I'm sorry," said the little girl. "I only borrowed it."
"That was very naughty," Mervyn said, sternly.

The little girl, whose name was Belinda, explained that she had wanted to find a spell that would turn her cousin Matilda's dress blue.

"But it hasn't worked," she sighed.
"It has," said Mervyn. "Only it was the *moon* you turned blue!"
Belinda looked very upset.
"Never mind," Mervyn went on. "I'm sure you've learned your lesson and won't take other people's things again!"

Mervyn leafed through his book and quickly found the spell to turn things back to normal.
"It's working!" the moon cheered. "Well done, Mervyn. And to show the girls there's no hard feelings, why don't you make Matilda's dress blue. But *properly* this time!"
"That's a good idea," agreed Mervyn.
The girls were delighted.
"Ooh, thank you, Mervyn!" they cheered.

Peggy's cosy nest

1 — Peggy Pigeon lived in the city in a nest made of thin twigs. This nest was quite cosy in the summer, but now the cold winter winds were starting to blow.

2 — Peggy watched the people hurrying by. They were all wrapped up warmly against the cold. "I wish I had a warm coat," thought Peggy, and she shivered.

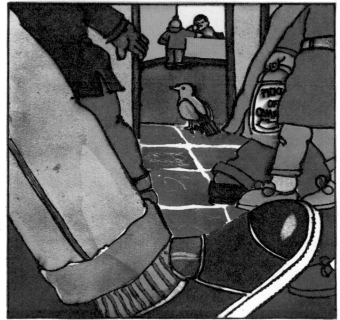

3 — Peggy flew down to the pavement to peck at some food. Just at that moment, a bus dropped off lots of people. "Help!" cheeped Peggy. "I'll be trampled!"

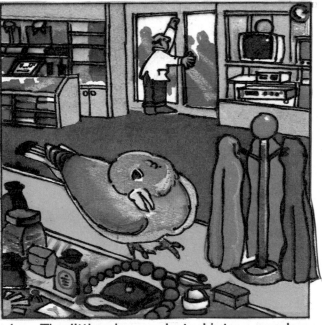

4 — The little pigeon darted into a nearby shop. "It's lovely and warm in here," she thought. She didn't notice the storekeeper closing the shop.

5 — Peggy didn't mind being locked in the shop, however. She set off to explore. Her first find was a cosy scarf. Peggy tried it on. "That looks silly!" she giggled.

6 — Then Peggy flew off to the wool department. "I could use some of this wool," she thought. Peggy picked some strands and put them in a little bag she found.

7 — Peggy's next stop was the toy department. The little pigeon pressed a button on a robot and it started to walk. Peggy *did* get a fright.

8 — Peggy thought the robot was chasing her. She jumped away from it and fell into a teddy bear's lap. The pigeon was glad *he* didn't get up and chase her!

9 — The little pigeon was tired out by this time. She curled up on the teddy's lap, clutching her precious bag of wool, and fell asleep, dreaming about a cosy nest.

10 — Next morning, Peggy left the shop as soon as it opened, carrying her wool. There were so many people in the shop, that no one saw her hurrying out through the door.

11 — Peggy flew back to her nest and lined it with the wool from the shop. "That's better," she sighed. "I won't mind the winter, now I've got a woolly nest."

Dusty finds a friend

DUSTY, the little ginger kitten, rolled over and over in the barn. He was chasing his tail.

"Oh, Dusty!" sighed his mother. "Why can't you go and play somewhere else! Your brothers and sisters are trying to have a little sleep."

"Sorry, Mummy!" said Dusty. "But I only want to play."

"I know," smiled Mummy. "You are always ready for a game. Go outside and see if you can find someone to play with."

"Good idea," agreed Dusty. And he scurried off at once.

Outside, in the farmyard, Dusty couldn't see anyone going about. The kitten crossed the yard and made his way over to Farmer Brown's house.

There was still no sign of anyone. Farmer Brown was busy in the fields and his wife was making butter in the dairy. Even Farmer Brown's daughter, Helen, was nowhere to be seen.

"Never mind," he sighed. "I'm sure to find someone who wants to play with me."

Beside the farmhouse was a kennel, where Shep, the farmer's dog, lived.

"I wonder if Shep would like to play a game?" thought Dusty.

Well, Shep had been very busy that morning, rounding up sheep, and all he wanted to do now was to sleep.

Little Dusty crept up to the dog — and pounced on his tail.

"Hey!" Shep yelled.

"Sorry," said Dusty. "But I only wanted to play."

"Well, go and play somewhere else," said Shep sternly.

Sadly, Dusty trotted off down the lane.

At last, he came to the pond.

"Oh, good!" thought Dusty, when he caught sight of Mother Duck and her little, fluffy ducklings. "Now I've found some playmates."

The ducklings were learning to swim and they didn't want to get out of the water to play with Dusty.

"*You* come in and join us," they said.

But, when Dusty dipped his paw into the water, it felt very cold.

"No, thanks," said Dusty. "I don't think I want to swim today."

By now, Dusty was feeling really miserable. He decided to go back to the farm.

"I'll just have to go to sleep in the barn with my brothers and sisters," he sighed. "No one wants to play with me."

As Dusty got near the farm, he heard voices.

"I know one of those voices," thought Dusty. "It's Helen, the farmer's daughter."

Dusty hurried over to the garden where Helen was playing with her chum, Louise.

When Dusty saw that the girls were playing with a ball, he ran over and pounced on it, purring happily.

"What a cute kitten!" cried Louise. "What's his name?"

"He's called Dusty," said Helen. "He's always getting into mischief. I think he wants to play."

So the girls let Dusty join in with their games for the rest of the afternoon.

Later, when Louise's mummy came to collect her, Farmer Brown said Louise could keep Dusty.

Luckily, Louise's mummy said, "Yes."

"Oh, thank you!" cried Louise. "I promise I'll take good care of Dusty. I'll play with him every day."

"That's great!" purred Dusty. "I've found a playmate at last. I'm the happiest kitten in the world!"

Fishing

MY daddy's brought me fishing with
   My rod, and line, and folding stool.
We're sitting on the riverbank;
   Inside the wood, just where it's cool.

We listen for the hidden birds
   To sing their songs from trees so tall,
I love to try to guess their names.
   My daddy seems to know them all.

The river flows by, clear and fresh,
   And swirls along towards the weir.
I keep quite still, and watch for trout
   That swim so swiftly, and so near!

I'd like to touch the sunbeams that
   Are shining on the giant fern.
Their light is colouring with gold
   Each branch, and plant, and leaf in turn.

Why, there's a tiny water vole!
   He sniffs the air, his eyes so bright.
But wait! What's tugging at my line?
   A fish! At last, I've got a bite!

A surprise for Fenella

FENELLA FAIRY shivered and pulled a woollen shawl around her shoulders.

"Oh, dear!" she sobbed. "It's so dark and cold in this cottage."

Fenella had moved into the cottage during the warm summer months. But now the winter winds had arrived and Fenella began to feel unhappy in her cottage.

A draught blew through a broken window and made Fenella shiver again.

"I'll light a big log fire to keep me warm," Fenella decided.

However, the strong draughts soon blew out the fire.

Fenella went to visit her kind friend, Maxie Mole. He invited Fenella into his cosy, bright burrow, where he gave her some hot tea and muffins. Then Fenella told Maxie how unhappy she was in her cold cottage.

"Let's go and find a new house for you to live in, Fenella," smiled Maxie.

There were three houses for sale in Bramble Forest. Maxie and Fenella set off to see them. The first house they came across was a small toadstool house which had belonged to Sammy Spider.

"It's far too small," sighed Fenella. "I would bump my head, every time I went through the doorway."

So Maxie and Fenella carried on walking through the forest, until they came to the second house which was for sale. It belonged to Ollie Otter.

He invited Fenella inside to see his home.

"But I'm afraid that my house wouldn't be at all suitable for *you* to live in," he told Fenella.

Fenella had to agree with him, when she saw that a river ran all the way through Ollie's house!

"Kenny Kingfisher's house is also for sale. Why don't you visit him?" suggested Ollie.

When Fenella arrived at Kenny Kingfisher's address, she was dismayed to see that his house was built high up in a tree.

Fenella carefully climbed up the tree. When she finally reached Kenny's house, she was exhausted.

"Do you like my home, Fenella?" asked Kenny.

"Oh, yes," Fenella replied, peering inside. "But I could never climb up and down this tall tree every day."

"Hop on to my back and I will fly you back to your old cottage, Fenella," Kenny smiled, kindly.

Soon, they came to Fenella's cottage. But what a *wonderful* surprise lay in store for Fenella when she opened her cottage door.

The rooms no longer felt cold, because Ollie Otter had repaired the split woodwork and broken windows. Now the wind wouldn't be able to bother Fenella. Ollie had also hung some colourful pictures to brighten up the walls.

Maxie Mole had made pretty patterned covers for Fenella's old sofa. He had placed bright cushions on the couch and hung curtains over the repaired windows.

"Oh, thank you," Fenella gasped, in delight. "Now my old, draughty cottage is the cosiest house in all the woodland!"

Kandy Kangaroo

1 — Kandy, the baby kangaroo, lived in the Australian outback with his mother and lots of other kangaroos. Kandy loved to play with all his friends.

2 — Being a kangaroo, Kandy was very good at jumping. So the two games he liked best were leap-frog and long-jump! Kandy could have played them all day.

3 — But Kandy was younger than the rest of his friends and had to go to bed earlier than them. "Aw, Mum!" he wailed, when she called him for bed. "I'm not tired."

4 — "You're still a baby," Kandy's mother told him. "You need your sleep." "I'll show Mum I'm grown up," Kandy thought. "I'll have an adventure."

5 — Kandy bounded away from his mother. A little way along the track, he met a wombat. "Please help me!" she sobbed and pointed to a bush.

6 — Kandy looked at the bush. He saw two feet poking out! It was Mrs Wombat's son and he was stuck. Kandy pulled out the little wombat. "Hooray!" cheered Mrs Wombat.

7 — Mrs Wombat was so grateful to Kandy for his help that she gave him a beautiful, shiny pebble as a thank you present. Kandy was very pleased with it

8 — Kandy said good-bye to his wombat friends and set off again. Soon, he saw a truck coming towards him. "Another adventure!" Kandy cheered.

9 — The truck stopped and a man and boy got out. "Look, Bruce," said the man. "It's a kangaroo." "He shouldn't be here by himself," said Bruce.

10 — Then Bruce remembered he had seen kangaroos not far away. "He must belong with them," he told his father. "Let's take him back then," the man said, with a smile.

11 — Kandy sat up proudly, as he was driven back to his mother. Kandy *did* enjoy the ride in the truck. Then Bruce let Kandy keep his hat as a souvenir!

12 — Kandy ran to his mother. "I've had an adventure!" he said. "I don't need to go to bed early any more." But then Kandy yawned. "Yes, you do!" chuckled Mummy.

Sea-side puzzles

Colour this picture with your paints or crayons, then find six starfish hidden on these pages.

Try to spot six differences between these two pictures of Pete the porpoise.

Help Sailor Ted through the maze to reach his ship.

5 **6**

4

7

14

3

15
8 **13** **17**

16

9 **12**
18

2
11 **19**

10

20

1

Join the dots to see who this is.

Which two of these seagulls are exactly alike?

Can you tell which of these anchors is tied to the boat?

B **C**

Answer:- C.

N B
A C I

Unscramble the jumbled letters to find out where the captain lives. Answer:- CABIN.

Ring-a-ling Rosie

Rosie, the little, green alarm clock, smiled happily, as she watched her owner, Melissa, packing her toys.

"We're moving house," Melissa told the toys.

Rosie *was* excited.

In fact, she was so excited, she began to ring loudly.

Ring-a-ling-a-ling!
Ring-a-ling-a-ling!

Poor Harvey, the dog, jumped up in the air. He had been sleeping in his basket, but the clock woke him up!

Harvey was so cross, he reached out his paw and knocked the alarm clock off the shelf.

The little clock fell down the back of Melissa's book-shelf.

Melissa didn't notice this. So, when she had finished packing away her toys, she left the room without realising the clock had been left behind.

"Oh, no!" Rosie cried.

The green alarm clock began to wriggle about.

At last, she managed to free herself from the back of the shelf.

"Even Harvey has gone without me," sighed the clock, when she looked around the room.

Carefully, Rosie made her way out of Melissa's room.

"However am I going to get down the stairs?" she wondered. "I'll have to go very slowly, in case I fall."

So, the alarm clock jumped down on to the first step.

But, oh dear! Rosie lost her balance and toppled down the rest of the stairs.

"Ah!" cried the clock. "Somebody help me."

But there was no one in the house. They were all outside, helping to load up the furniture removal van.

At last, the little clock came to rest on the hall floor.

"Phew! That was terrible!" puffed Rosie. She noticed the little legs she used to stand on had broken off during the fall.

Just then, the cat flap in the door lifted up and Harvey, the dog, peeped in.

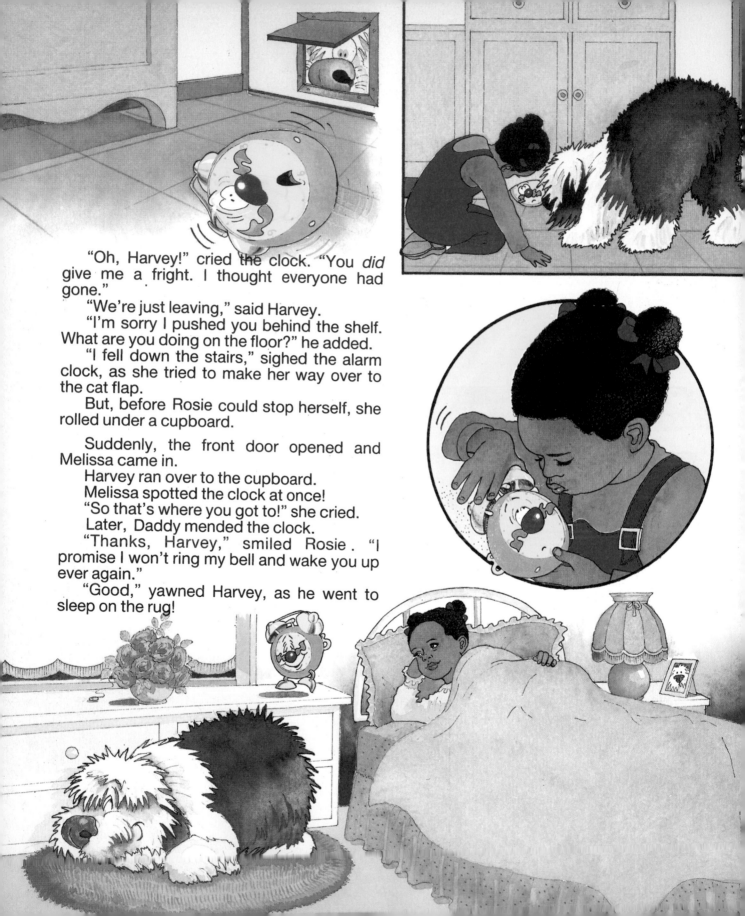

"Oh, Harvey!" cried the clock. "You *did* give me a fright. I thought everyone had gone."

"We're just leaving," said Harvey.

"I'm sorry I pushed you behind the shelf. What are you doing on the floor?" he added.

"I fell down the stairs," sighed the alarm clock, as she tried to make her way over to the cat flap.

But, before Rosie could stop herself, she rolled under a cupboard.

Suddenly, the front door opened and Melissa came in.

Harvey ran over to the cupboard.

Melissa spotted the clock at once!

"So that's where you got to!" she cried.

Later, Daddy mended the clock.

"Thanks, Harvey," smiled Rosie . "I promise I won't ring my bell and wake you up ever again."

"Good," yawned Harvey, as he went to sleep on the rug!

The ladybird

YOU'LL find the tiny ladybird,
So pretty and so small,
Resting upon a garden shrub,
Or on a fence or wall.

She is black and red and shiny,
But try to count her spots.
Some ladybirds have only two,
And some have lots and lots!

Follow these simple
steps and draw a ladybird.

Can you tell which two
of these ladybirds are
exactly alike?

You will see her busy working,
Through all the summer hours,
Getting rid of all the creatures
That spoil our plants and flowers.

But, when the winter comes again,
And gardens start to freeze,
She will snuggle down, so cosy,
Under the bark of trees.

You can colour this picture below,
using your paints or crayons.

Pam's garden party

1 — Pam was playing in her garden, one afternoon, when Mummy called her over. "Don't go near the bushes," she said. "There are blackbirds nesting there."

2 — Every morning, the little girl asked Mummy if the eggs in the blackbirds' nest had hatched. But Mummy always replied, "No, Pam, not yet."

3 — Pam had almost given up hope of ever seeing any baby blackbirds. Then, one morning, she heard chirping noises from the bottom of the garden.

4 — She hurried quickly across the lawn and peered carefully through the bushes. There, sure enough, she saw a little head popping out of one of the eggs.

5 — From then on, Pam decided to help the garden visitors. She left out crumbs for them, every morning, so that they could feed their young.

6 — As she was going into the kitchen, one day, however, Pam saw one of the baby birds on a high cupboard. "It must have flown in the window," she gasped. "I'll try to rescue it."

7 — Pam heard birds chirping anxiously at the back door. The blackbird parents had seen the baby bird flying in the window and were trying to call it back outside to the nest.

8 — The little girl thought she would use breadcrumbs to tempt the baby bird outside. But all she did was frighten the parent birds away.

10 — Ever so carefully, Mummy carried the bird outside and set it down on the grass. Pam cried with delight as the mother and father birds came swooping down to collect their baby.

9 — At last, Mummy climbed up on a chair to reach the cupboard. She lifted the baby bird gently in her hands, trying not to frighten it.

11 — A few moments later, the rest of the blackbird family came flying down from the nest to join in the celebration on the lawn. The little birds fluttered around happily.

12 — "Listen to them chirping," said Pam's mummy. "Just as if they're singing to thank us." "I'll fetch more bread," cried Pam. "This is like a garden party!"

Tiny and Tim

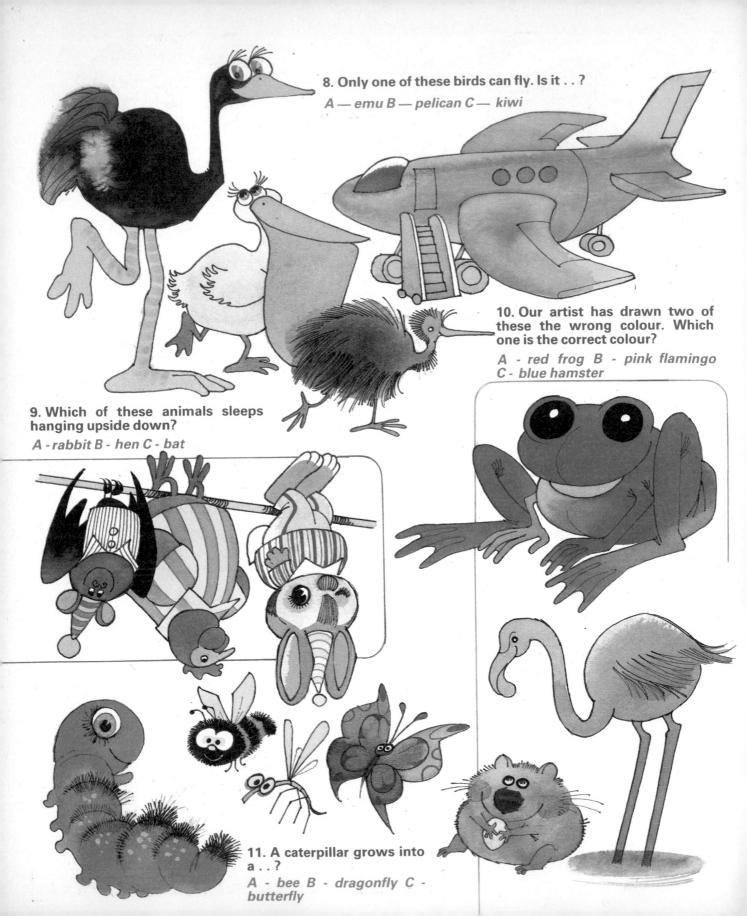

8. Only one of these birds can fly. Is it . . ?

A — emu B — pelican C — kiwi

10. Our artist has drawn two of these the wrong colour. Which one is the correct colour?

A - red frog B - pink flamingo C - blue hamster

9. Which of these animals sleeps hanging upside down?

A - rabbit B - hen C - bat

11. A caterpillar grows into a . . ?

A - bee B - dragonfly C - butterfly